MERRY CHRISTMAS, BUGS!

by David A. Carter

Ready-to-Read

Simon Spotlight

New York   London   Toronto   Sydney   New Delhi

SIMON SPOTLIGHT
An imprint of Simon & Schuster Children's Publishing Division
1230 Avenue of the Americas, New York, New York 10020
This Simon Spotlight edition September 2014
Copyright © 2014 by David A. Carter
All rights reserved, including the right of reproduction in whole or in part in any form.
SIMON SPOTLIGHT, READY-TO-READ, and colophon are registered trademarks of Simon
& Schuster, Inc.For information about special discounts for bulk purchases, please contact Simon
& Schuster Special Sales at 1-866-506-1949 or business@simonandschuster.com.
The Simon & Schuster Speakers Bureau can bring authors to your live event. For more information
or to book an event contact the Simon & Schuster Speakers Bureau at 1-866-248-3049 or
visit our website at www.simonspeakers.com.
Manufactured in the United States of America 0814 LAK
Designed by Chani Yammer
10 9 8 7 6 5 4 3 2 1
Library of Congress Cataloging-in-Publication Data
Carter, David A., author, illustrator.
Merry Christmas, bugs! / by David A. Carter. — First edition.
pages cm. — (Ready-to-read)
1. Pop-up books—Specimens. I. Title.
PZ7.C2429Mer 2014
[E]—dc23
2013041319
ISBN 978-1-4424-9506-7 (pbk)
ISBN 978-1-4424-9507-4 (hc)
ISBN 978-1-4424-9508-1 (eBook)

Jingle Bugs, Jingle Bugs! Christmas is almost here!

Snowflake Bugs
frost the windows.
Skating Bugs dance on ice.
Snowball Bugs
zoom around.

The Bugs are excited
for the holidays.
Christmas cheer abounds!

But Bitsy Bee is worried.
She has given all of her gifts
but one.

The last is for her friend
Busy Bug,
and she wants it to be
extra fun.

So Bitsy goes to town
to pick something that is
just right.

She wonders what
she will find for her friend.
A pair of shoes?
A giant cookie?
A whirly-twirly kite?

She decides to stop
at the pet store.

The puppy is too loud.
The turtle is too slow.
The kitten is too scratchy.
So Bitsy looks some more.

Bitsy goes in to
the magic shop.
It is filled with
many fun things.

A tricky Wand Bug?
A smiling Top-Hat Bug?
A Juggling Bug who sings?

Bitsy shakes her head.
Then she continues on.

She is running out of time.
Christmas Eve
is almost gone!

Bitsy thinks all hope is lost, then she looks at the bookstore windows.

She suddenly has an idea.
It is perfect, she knows!

Bitsy runs to her house,
where Mama Bug is
making tea.

She sits at her little desk
and begins to write
the story of two best friends,
Busy Bug and Bitsy Bee!

Then she draws
some pictures to go along
with the tale.

On Christmas morning,
Busy Bug arrives.
In his hand he has a pail!

Busy gives Bitsy
a pretty flower
he planted just for her.

Then the friends
read Bitsy's story
under the tree together.

Merry Christmas, Bugs!